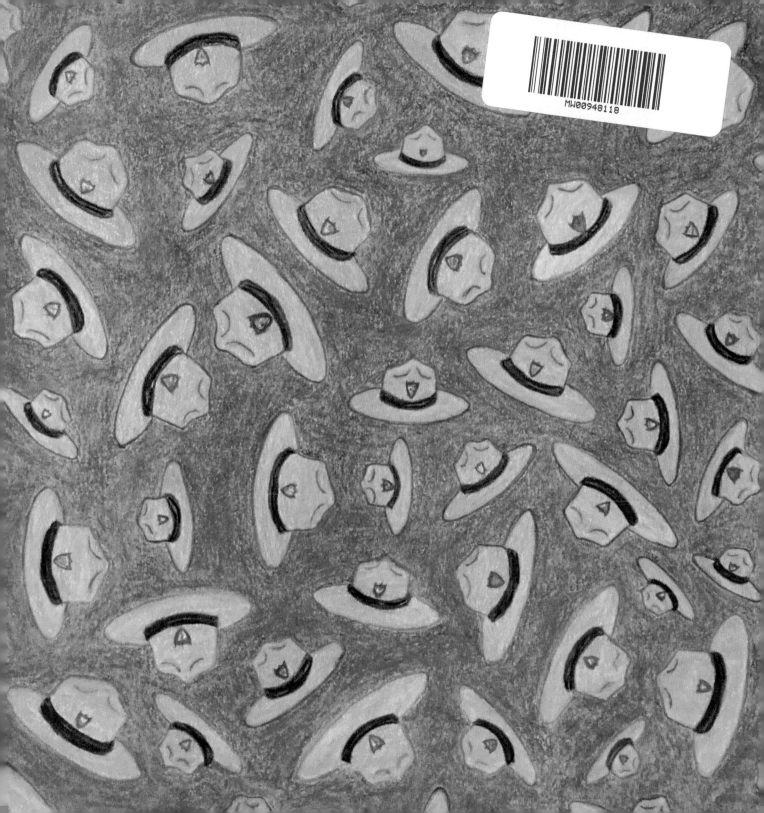

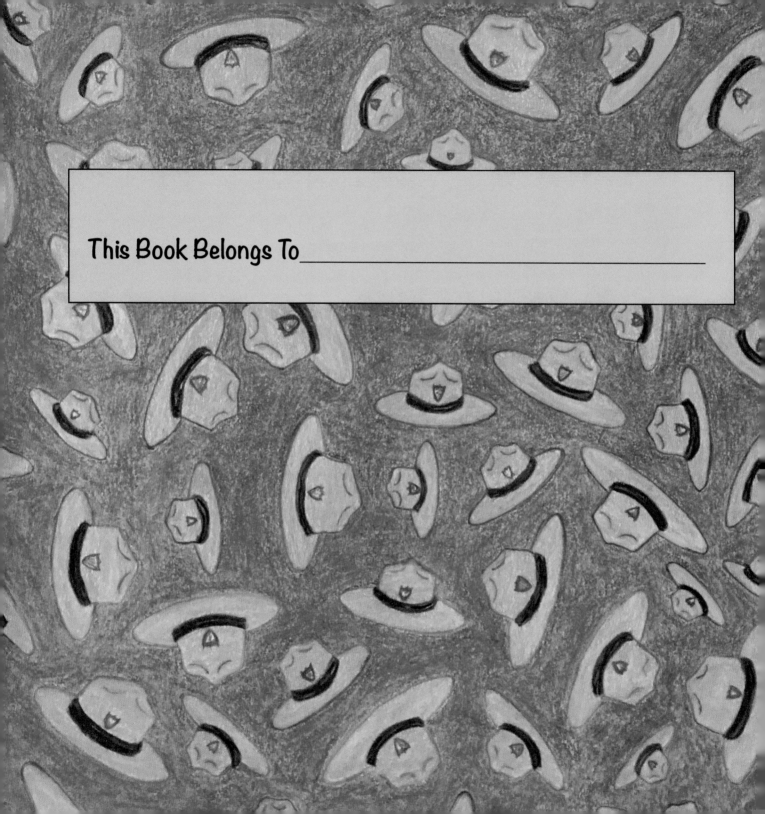

This Book Belongs To_____

Wilber's Very First Vacation

One warm summer day, Wilber's little boy Oliver said, "Guess what Wilber? We are going on vacation to a very special place." Wilber started jumping with excitement, but he wondered what "vacation" was. And where was "someplace special?"

Early the next morning, Oliver said, "Let's get ready to go on your 'very' first vacation, Wilber." The two buddies packed everything they needed for a week-long camping trip.

Wilber and Oliver lived by a small forest, but this was going to be different. They were going to a very big forest with tall pine trees, way up high in the mountains.

They went to the bus station and climbed aboard a big bus that would take them to a state called Colorado.

MOOSE TRACKS

MOOSE TRACKS

When the two buddies got to the town of Estes Park in Colorado, they got off the big bus. They had to wait just a short while.

"That's our bus Wilber"

ESTES PARK COLORADO

Soon, a smaller bus pulled up and they jumped on. This was a park bus that was going to take them into the National Park.

PARK BUS

BUS STOP

JEWELRY   T-SHIRTS

OPEN

At the entrance to the park, Oliver read a very big sign to Wilber that said, "Stoney Mountain National Park."

Wilber and Oliver could smell the fresh mountain air. The weather was perfect for camping and spending time outdoors. The fresh air and the smell of pine from the evergreen trees made Wilber giddy and he smiled with delight! There was so much to see and so many things they were going to do.

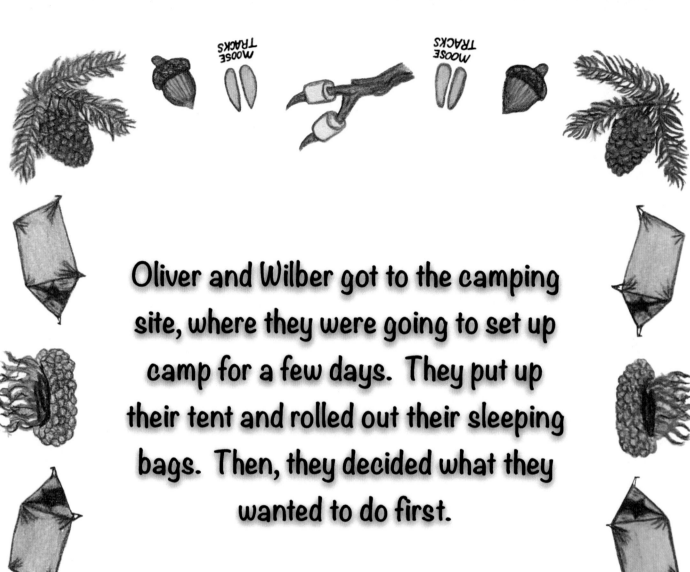

Oliver and Wilber got to the camping site, where they were going to set up camp for a few days. They put up their tent and rolled out their sleeping bags. Then, they decided what they wanted to do first.

MOOSE
TRACKS

MOOSE
TRACKS

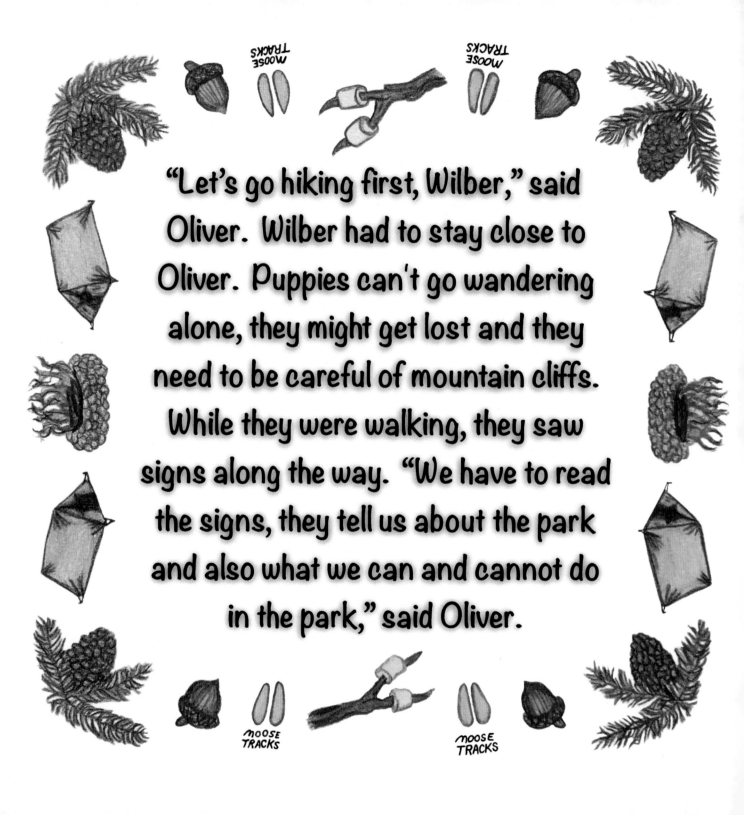

"Let's go hiking first, Wilber," said Oliver. Wilber had to stay close to Oliver. Puppies can't go wandering alone, they might get lost and they need to be careful of mountain cliffs. While they were walking, they saw signs along the way. "We have to read the signs, they tell us about the park and also what we can and cannot do in the park," said Oliver.

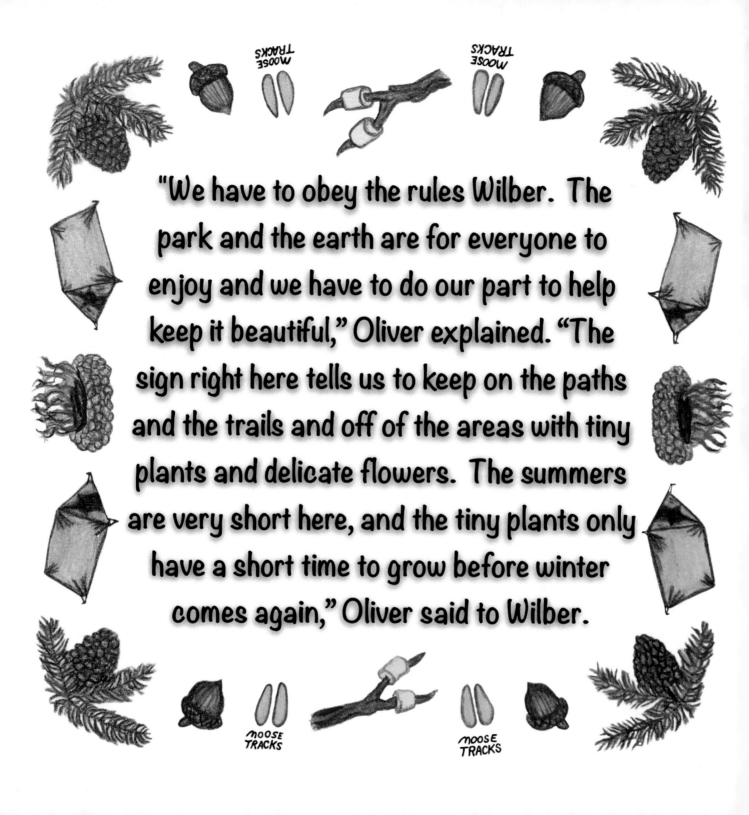

"We have to obey the rules Wilber. The park and the earth are for everyone to enjoy and we have to do our part to help keep it beautiful," Oliver explained. "The sign right here tells us to keep on the paths and the trails and off of the areas with tiny plants and delicate flowers. The summers are very short here, and the tiny plants only have a short time to grow before winter comes again," Oliver said to Wilber.

MOOSE TRACKS

MOOSE TRACKS

"That sign over there, says that we have to stay back and look at the wildlife from a distance so we don't bother the wild animals," said Oliver. "But most of all, we don't want to get hurt by the animals. This is their home, not ours. I'm so glad we get to visit the park and enjoy all the nature and wildlife here."

MOOSE TRACKS

MOOSE TRACKS

"The park rangers take care of the park and the animals here. They help all of us and the trees and plant life too," Oliver said.

Oliver and Wilber had a lot of fun watching the animals and taking many pictures of all of the wonders of the park.

Oliver and Wilber used binoculars to see the animals from a distance so they wouldn't frighten them or scare them away. They saw beautiful song birds and Bald Eagles flying high in the sky. There were bears with their little ones, moose and all sorts of other animals too.

MOOSE
TRACKS

MOOSE
TRACKS

There were rivers and streams that
made wonderful gurgling sounds as the
water rushed down the mountains and
into the lakes. The water was so clear
and blue that they could see the fish
swimming on the bottom of the lake.
And the two friends decided that fishing
in the lake was a great way to spend
their last day of vacation.

MOOSE
TRACKS

MOOSE
TRACKS

They had such a great time, but sadly, the week was almost over and it was time to pack up their things and head home. They got back on the bus that would take them out of the park. As they were leaving, Oliver said, "Goodbye," to the park and promised Wilber that they would visit the park again next summer.

The two buddies got off the small bus, back at the town of Estes Park, where they had climbed on the bus a few days before. They waited for the big bus and soon it pulled up. Wilber and Oliver got on and it took them on the long ride back home. The two buddies were so tired that they fell asleep for a while during the ride home.

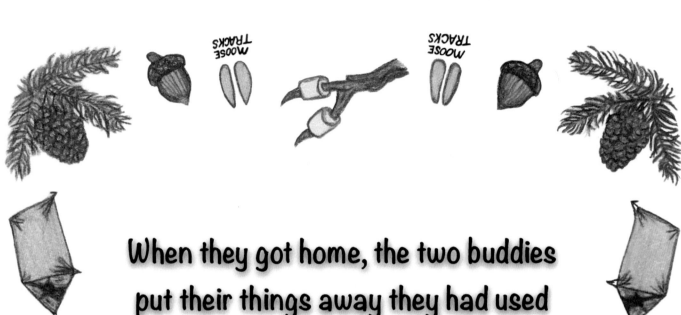

When they got home, the two buddies put their things away they had used for camping. Oliver and Wilber remembered all of the fun they had. And they looked at all of the great pictures they had taken of their special vacation.

Oliver said to Wilber, "We can be proud of ourselves for obeying all of the park rules. We will be good next year when we visit the park too!"

Oliver said with a big smile, "We had such a fun time!" Wilber nodded his head to show he agreed and Oliver gave him a great big hug!

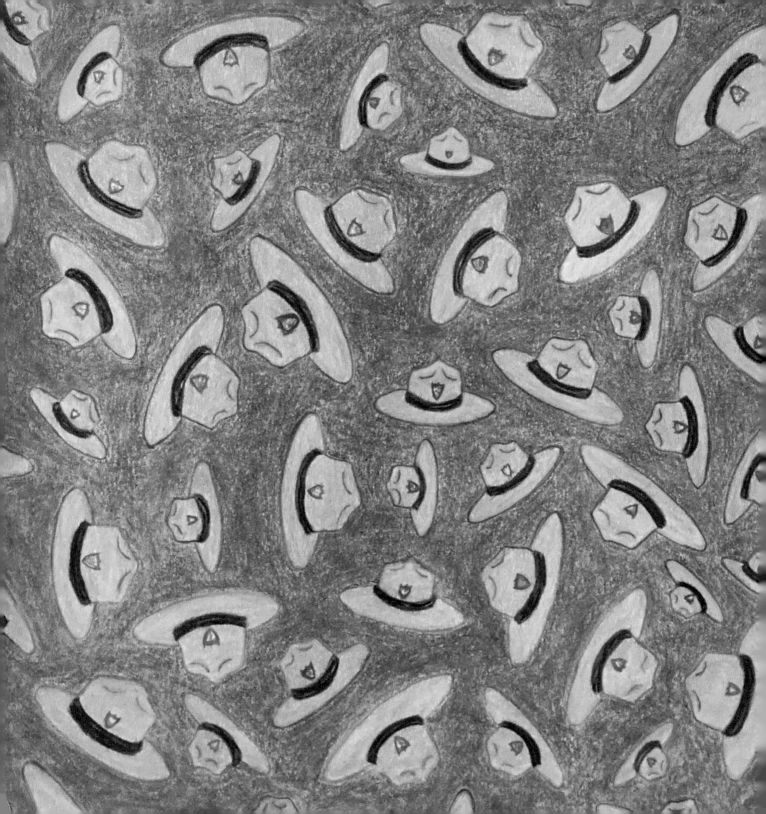

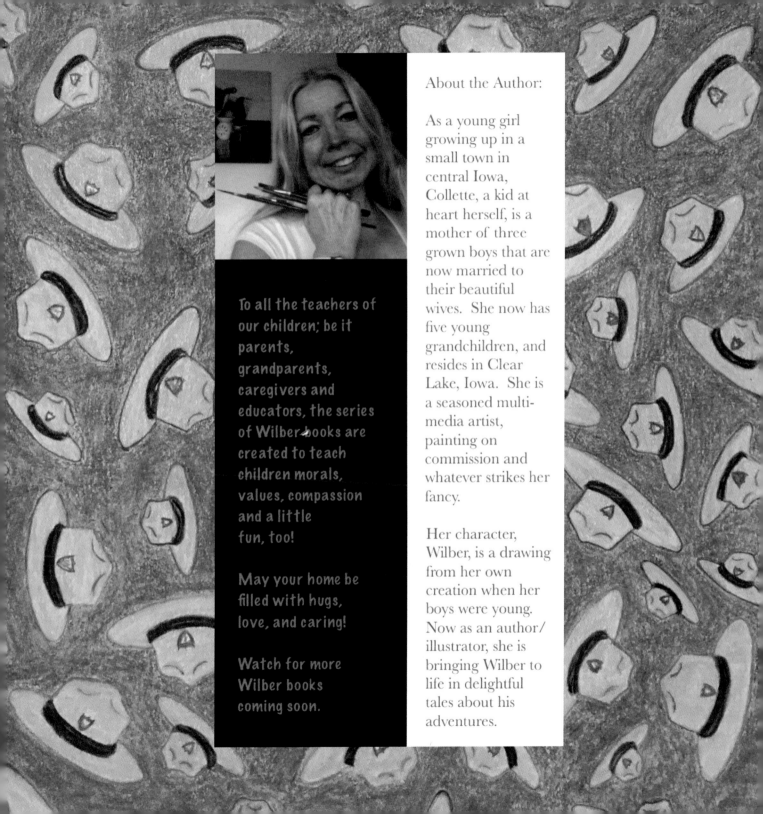

To all the teachers of
our children; be it
parents,
grandparents,
caregivers and
educators, the series
of Wilber books are
created to teach
children morals,
values, compassion
and a little
fun, too!

May your home be
filled with hugs,
love, and caring!

Watch for more
Wilber books
coming soon.

About the Author:

As a young girl
growing up in a
small town in
central Iowa,
Collette, a kid at
heart herself, is a
mother of three
grown boys that are
now married to
their beautiful
wives. She now has
five young
grandchildren, and
resides in Clear
Lake, Iowa. She is
a seasoned multi-
media artist,
painting on
commission and
whatever strikes her
fancy.

Her character,
Wilber, is a drawing
from her own
creation when her
boys were young.
Now as an author/
illustrator, she is
bringing Wilber to
life in delightful
tales about his
adventures.

10843563R00029

Made in the USA
Monee, IL
07 September 2019